I0630911

STUNG!

A Theophilus Hornby Mystery

L. Edward Dixon

eucatastrophe press
an imprint of Energion Publications
Cantonment, Florida
2024

Cover art by Ruth Bloom. The face on Dr. Hornby is that of her dear husband John who is now with the Lord.
Addition Cover Design: Erin McClellan

ISBN: 978-1-63199-903-1
eISBN: 978-1-63199-904-8

eucatastrophe press
An imprint of Energion Publications
1241 Conference Rd
Cantonment, FL 32533

energion.com
pubs@energion.com

(850) 525-3916

There it is again — a very faint sound. Or is it my imagination? Is it coming from my radio? Can't be. Radio's not even on. Is it possible?

He continued driving. He dreaded that sound more than just about any other on earth. Goosebumps immediately began to rise on his muscular, tattooed arms, giving him a chill as he listened hard. But the buzzing became louder and more terrifying. The sweat started to bead on his tanned forehead. He felt himself plunging into full-fledged panic.

"Oh, no! Please, God! It can't be!," he said out loud to himself. But all doubt was gone. And there was nothing he could do about it.

The luxury sedan swerved left and then right as he tried to elude the intruder. "I hate these things!", he screamed a curse as he tried to keep the steering wheel straight.

But his terror overcame his caution as he sought in vain to fend off the unwelcome encounter that was destined — some might say predestined — to happen. The guardrail was no match for the 3715 pound Lexus as it tore through it like it was made out of paper. His blood-curdling scream was not heard by anyone on this lonely stretch of highway. At his rate of speed, the trajectory took him 25 feet past the crumpled guardrail, plunging him into a several second silence where the only sound was the rushing wind framing his desperate cry of "Noooooo!" Crashing into the rocky creek bed 150 feet below assured an unsurvivable event.

Ch. 2

At the bottom of the small canyon, the Lexus was one crumpled mess. "What a waste of a hundred-thousand dollar car!", Officer Bondo said out loud.

"Maybe you ought to care about the dead body we'll need to pry out of that hundred-thousand dollar car, Bondo!", snapped Sargent Sanders.

After rappelling down the sheer cliff, the EMT's worked with the jaws of life to pop open the driver's door and it became immediately apparent that there was no life left in its occupant.

"A dozen air bags couldn't have saved that guy," commented one of the EMT's. They strapped the body on the gurney, signaling their comrades to pull up the corpse. Several times the gurney slammed against the rocks and the rescue workers winced at each occurrence. But the victim didn't mind. Hours before he had departed this vale of tears.

"Hey, I know that guy!," shouted another rescue worker. "That's Bubba Delvaney, the crime boss from Chicago!"

Delvaney had recently been found not guilty on racketeering and murder charges. Several key witnesses had disappeared and the Federal Prosecutor Diane Miller's case had crumbled before her eyes.

Delvaney had left the courtroom with a smirk, and then celebrated his legal victory with his friends at Pontefiori's Family Restaurant. Feasting on some of his favorite Italian dishes, including pasta primavera, chicken Saltimbocca, and fettuccine Alfredo, he slapped his lawyer on the back and offered a toast to the legal profession.

Three and a-half hours later Fernando, a six-foot-six former NFL tackle who faithfully served as Delvaney's assistant and bodyguard, asked, "Hey, boss? Want I should drive you home?"

"Nah," Delvaney said. "I didn't drink that much. I'll be okay." Okay was the last thing the crime boss would be. And those were the final words any human heard him say. Justice was now complete.

 # Ch. 3

Dr. Theophilus Hornby, Professor of Bible and Theology at Faithful Bible College, could hardly believe his luck. Well, "luck" was definitely the wrong word for a mostly-convinced Calvinist like himself, but he still felt "blessed." Hmmm, he thought to himself. I wonder if the word "blessed" is used by Christians like unsaved people use the word "luck"?

Theo, as his friends called him, had just read the email from the college's president that the faculty meeting for that afternoon had been cancelled. Is there any greater news at the end of the school year, Hornby wondered, than not having to attend a faculty meeting? "I guess I'm the recipient of sovereign, blessed luck!", he chuckled to himself.

Faithful Bible College was located on forty beautiful acres of prime real estate in Western North Carolina, an area known for its spectrum of colors in the fall and its well-used ski slopes in the winter. Hornby had given up skiing for two reasons. He was, after all, seventy-two years old, with knees that reminded him of his age whenever he skied or played tennis with other senior faculty at FBC. And, he had lost one of his best friends to a skiing accident just six months before.

Loss seemed to mark Hornby's last several years. His only son Mark had vanished in Tibet as he had prepared to scale Mt. Everest with a climbing club from North Carolina. There had been a rash of kidnappings in that area of Nepal, but no group had made any ransom demands.

On the eve of his team's ascent, Mark had gone for a walk and did not return to the team's lodgings. The sheer pain of not knowing what had happened to his son had severely tested Hornby's faith, and he had had many angry and broken conversations with the Lord in prayer over his son's disappearance.

Losing his wife Eleanor to cancer two years before had been especially difficult for him. They had no sooner celebrated their 50th wedding anniversary than she was diagnosed. He missed Ellie terribly, but he had slowly found some comfort in the Lord and in the Lord's people.

Hornby sat in his old recliner and reminisced about Ellie. He remembered her trying to get rid of that recliner one Saturday by saying, "Theo, it's old and ragged and has long out-lived its usefulness! Let's get you a new one." Hornby responded by saying, "The same three things could be said about me!" They laughed and laughed -- but he got to keep his comfortable, form-fitting, cracked leather recliner. Hornby thought to himself that sometimes where one thinks deep thoughts is almost as important as the thoughts themselves.

Settling into his recliner with his microwaved Hungry-Man TV dinner and his ice cold can of root beer from the kitchen, Hornby said to his cat Luther, "Let's see what's on the Classics channel." Luther was a twelve-year-old Persian who was about 10 pounds overweight and moved slowly, deliberately, and, if it had a choice, infrequently. Luther was helped by Hornby up onto the foot of the recliner and his deep-throated purring was almost like the vibrator on one of those fancy new LazyBoys. Luther knew that Hornby would leave a little of the gravy and the meat and maybe some of the potatoes for him to enjoy after Hornby was finished.

"Let's see what's on the Classics channel" meant that Hornby was going to watch an ancient episode of "Columbo," the detective show starring the bumbling one-eyed actor Peter Falk. Falk had had his right eye surgically removed in real life due to cancer when he was only three.

"Oh, good," said Hornby. "The show's just starting. 'The Case of the Overweight Mistress.' Hmmm, Luther, I wonder if I have seen this one before?" Hornby had probably seen all 68 episodes of the show, but he always fell asleep in his recliner just before the show's conclusion. Tonight was no exception. When he woke up, Hornby said, "Luther, I can't believe it! I fell asleep! How did the mystery get solved by Columbo? Oh, well, I guess I'll have to watch this one again sometime."

Luther looked up from his corner of the recliner where he too had dozed off. His look seemed to say, "You're surprised you fell asleep? But it happens every night. Now, did I hear you say something about the remains of your TV dinner?"

Hornby put down the dinner plate for Luther to finish up what had been left of his meal. A few minutes later, after Luther had been out to do his business, the two tucked in, with Luther taking his customary spot at the foot of the bed, curled up and ready for a long night's rest.

Little did Hornby suspect that there would be a real-life mystery that would invade his world, a mystery for which Hornby would require two good eyes.

 # Ch. 4

Faithful Bible College was founded in 1941 by the Reverend Lawrence W. Clemons, an associate evangelist of D.L. Moody. FBC had only recently celebrated its 75th anniversary.

The school rightfully prided itself on its commitment to the authority of the Bible, the relevance of the Christian gospel, and the need to train young people in the skills they would require to serve Jesus in a post-Christian, and frequently anti-Christian, society.

I've never seen such a dedicated faculty, thought Dean Sean Miller to himself. They're not only excellent teachers, but they are paid so much less than they could earn at a secular university.

"Good morning, Dean Miller," said Bible professor Dr. Hornby.

"And a good morning to you too," responded Miller. "What classes do you have today, Theo?"

Dr. Miller knew full well that Hornby had two classes today — "Intro to Theology" and "Discipleship 101."

Hornby smiled and said, "Don't worry, Sean, I probably won't forget which class I'm teaching!"

This bit of repartee came from an incident a few months ago when Hornby began his class lecturing on the Hebrew grammar used in the Dead Sea Scrolls to a freshman class in Church History. After a few minutes, a young coed raised her hand and said, "Uh, Dr. Hornby, will we need to know this for our midterm in, uh, church history next week?", Hornby turned scarlet and put aside his Old Testament lecture notebook.

"Hmmm. Sorry about that, students! I guess my old age is catching up with me."

The students laughed and looked at him with deep affection. They knew how much he cared about them and how hard he worked to make his lectures not only interesting, but practical. He had only missed one week of classes after his beloved Eleanor had passed away from breast cancer.

Faithful Bible College's classes were almost done for the Spring semester. The student body numbered only about 150, so it was fairly easy for the nine members of the faculty to learn almost all of the students' names.

Although every student had to major in Bible, there were several minors at FBC that students could pursue. Dr. Rick Nation was the department chair of political science and math minors. Mrs. Gertrude Kominsky was in charge of the English and American Literature minors. Dr. Mortimer Sandover supervised several adjunct teachers in the Business Administration program. Dr. Warren Peace oversaw historical studies and Dr. Hornby was the head of the Bible/ Theology studies.

All the teachers were committed Evangelical Christians and their camaraderie was, to Hornby, one of the best parts of teaching at FBC. Each could have made more money teaching elsewhere, but FBC, though small, challenged their trust in the Lord to provide for the school and gave them great freedom in administering their various programs.

Hornby enjoyed the bantering, the give-and-take, between the faculty members. All seemed to relish teasing each other, some playing practical jokes, others poking fun at each other's foibles. Although it was never said, they simply loved each other and their role in the ministry of training a new generation of church leaders at FBC.

"Say, Mortimer," Rick Nation said one day in the faculty lounge.

"Yes, Rick?"

"You run our Business Administration program, right?"

"You know that I do, Dr. Nation. Why do you ask?"

"Well, Mort, I heard that you bounced a check at the local Seven- Eleven last Friday! You'd think the head of the Business Administration department would know how much money he had in his personal checking account!" Nation laughed, partly because Sandover had done the exact same thing the month before.

"Yep, I sure did," Sandover blushed as he began walking out of the faculty lounge. "But I heard that you actually misquoted Jesus the other day in your political science class."

"What? Never! What did you hear?"

"I heard you said that 'Jesus was a friend of Republicans and sinners,' misquoting Matthew 11. You really meant Democrats, right?" Mort laughed as he asked his question. Everyone knew that Nation was a committed member of the Democratic party, even though it sometimes presented a real challenge to his Christian convictions.

The students quickly picked up on the good natured teasing of the faculty, and weren't reluctant to follow their example. Hornby thought back to one Monday morning as he got to school for his 8 am "Intro to Theology" class. He went into his classroom, placed his hat on his desk, then went to make himself a cup of tea in his office.

He got a bit side-tracked and finally returned to the classroom by 8:12. No students. Everyone had left. They had assumed that class was cancelled. Hornby sent the class what was to him a strongly-worded email which read, "When my hat is on my desk, I am in the classroom and class is not CANCELLED!"

The next Monday Hornby got to the classroom a bit early, put his hat on his desk, then went to his office to make tea. He got back to the classroom at about five minutes after 8, only to find no students there, but 32 hats each nicely placed squarely on the students' desks.

Hornby laughed and laughed about that prank, remembering that he had pulled exactly the same stunt when he had been a student, earning the nickname "the Mad Hatter." "I guess what goes around comes around," he said to himself.

Hornby unlocked his office door on the second floor of the classroom building, sequentially turning on the five lamps in his office, his small waterfall planter, and his ancient cassette player. He hated the fluorescent overhead lights and almost never used them. Even though cassettes were an outdated medium, he had accumulated quite a collection over the years, his two favorites being B.B. King's "Greatest Hits" and the album "Chicago's Number One Singles." Hornby loved going to thrift stores and adding to his treasury for about a dime a cassette.

He looked around his office, once again purposing in his mind to get rid of the three boxes which had been on his floor for almost a year. I've got too many books and not enough room for them, he thought. He was gradually going through his collection and selling or giving away books to students to assist them in beginning their own libraries.

One shelf held multiple copies of the four books he himself had written over the last few years. Their titles included, "Anyone Searching for the Real Jesus?", a challenge to the so-called historical search for Jesus which often seemed to be nothing more than a liberal effort to discount the reliability of the four gospels. Hornby also had his autobiographical account of his trip to Turkey ten years before to search for Noah's ark, entitled "Where's the Ark Parked?" What a waste of time that trip was, he thought out loud, although he was fairly pleased with the title.

His third book was a memoir of his life with Ellie, including his daily journal of the last few months of her battle with cancer. "I Was Made to Love Her" was more than a Stevie Wonder song to Hornby. His latest book, written about a year ago, was a literary lark which he thoroughly enjoyed writing. Entitled "Calvin Had a Cat," the purposed author was John Calvin's cat Ulrich and its life with the famed Reformer. Hornby was fairly proud of this last book, for there was a lot of theology and history included in the "memories" of the Frenchman's feline. He had promised himself that any student who came to his office and commented on the books he had written would be given his or her choice of one of them for free.

Hornby worked hard to make his office a comfortable place for students to come and ask their questions, talk about their struggles, or just hang out. He had a large plaid couch on the right side as one entered the office, then his desk against the back windows, and then his small refrigerator and microwave. His office furnishings were completed by a year-old Lazyboy recliner FBC's board had purchased for him to honor his thirty years of teaching Bible and theology. It's not quite as comfortable as mine at home, he thought to himself, but I have been known to catch a few z's there before or after class.

His refrigerator was stocked with a pint of Half 'n half, a canister of Starbucks bold coffee, two six-packs of RC cola, and a package of MoonPies. Hornby had enjoyed an RC cola and a MoonPie (which consisted of a large marshmallow squished between two large chocolaty round cookies) as a child. A perfectly balanced lunch, he laughed to himself. He thought it his mission to share that dual treat with any student who came to visit, and more than a few had left with more energy than when they had come!

Down his hall, past the men's and ladies' bathrooms, was the faculty lounge. Someone early in FBC's history had fought against its creation. Apparently one of the board members, when the building was in the planning stages, had said, "We don't need a faculty lounge! The last thing our teachers should be doing is standing around drinking a bunch of coffee and shooting the breeze!"

Fortunately, that board member was outvoted and the lounge was created out of two spare offices with the wall between the rooms removed. A local furniture store had donated large leather couches, four overstuffed chairs, and beautiful hardwood coffee tables which displayed the faculty's recent publications. Oh, and the board person who objected to the lounge? He visited the lounge several times during the semester, observing how the teachers encouraged one another, prayed for each other, and brainstormed together about projects that would help FBC in its mission. He was convinced and showed his "conversion" by purchasing a top-of-the-line coffee machine and a year's supply of gourmet coffees and teas.

Hornby knew that the nine faculty could easily stay in their own offices getting ready for their classes, but the lounge drew them into a fellowship and community that no number of faculty meetings could ever create. And each was expected to spend at least a few minutes in the lounge after the school's daily chapel was over and before lunch. A teacher who was seen little in the lounge would be followed up by his or her colleagues to make sure things were going well. This was another perk of teaching at FBC.

 # Ch. 5

Detective Lance Ryland couldn't understand how Delvaney, whose blood alcohol level was below .08, could have simply driven his Lexus over a cliff. "It just doesn't make a lick of sense," he said out loud to himself. "Unless he was swerving to avoid a deer or something, one might think he purposely did himself in!"

A routine autopsy was done on Delvaney's body. Dr. Michael Stumpf was straightforward in his report. "No detectible injuries pre-mortem. No evidence of a stroke or a brain abnormality. Injuries consistent with a major car accident. Nothing unusual about the victim's death."

****

"What a fascinating read," John Smith thought to himself. He had hacked into the coroner's website and the post-mortem report on Delvaney. "Thankfully, they think it was an accident," he muttered. "Not true at all. Nor was this a murder or a suicide. It was a justifiable homicide. An execution. A judgment. A biblical judgment."

****

"Hey, Boss! You really think Bubba offed himself?!", asked Butch Milano, one of Mike Slaughter's "associates." Slaughter controlled most of the illegal drug enterprise and all of the prostitution rings in Chicago.

"No way, Butch," Milano said.

"Boss, Delvaney was just acquitted! He walks out of the restaurant after celebrating and then drives off a cliff. No skid marks. No evidence of another car banging into him."

"I know. I know. I think someone was after him. Who were his enemies? Track down his cell phone records. Did he call anybody before he croaked? Nobody just found 'not guilty' drives himself off a cliff!"

"I'll get right on it, Boss," Butch said.

Ch. 6

Monday afternoon was Hornby's day to go grocery shopping. His diet included more than tv dinners, but his level of absent-mindedness seemed to be increasing as the years rolled on. He would lose track of time, forget what he came to buy, or get caught up in a conversation about theology.

He was fond of saying, "Theology is not boring. Theologians are boring!" He tried his best to keep his lectures and class discussions relevant and practical and, well, interesting. He remembered his old friend Daryl Busby, a former colleague at a small Bible college in Canada, saying, "Surely it must be a sin to bore God's people with God's Word!"

Hornby was always ready to discuss doctrinal matters, because good doctrine, he believed, was solidly based in truth. And the truth will set you free, he thought to himself.

He remembered going grocery shopping one Monday afternoon when he met his plumber friend John Ensel who had also lost his wife to cancer. "Theo," John said, "got your list?"

"List? Oh, my. Nope. Forgot it again!", Hornby answered.

"Well, that's okay, my friend. Somedays without my Mary I find it hard to put one foot in front of the other. But we must, you know?"

"Yeah, I know," Hornby answered. "I know she's with the Lord, and her pain is gone, and she's probably so enamored with the Lord Jesus that she hardly even thinks about me down here."

"I'm not so sure about that, Theo," Ensel responded. But what do I know? I'm just a humble plumber, DR. Hornby!"

Hornby and Ensel loved poking fun at each other, especially about their different levels of education. "I'm not so sure how truly humble you are, John. I know that you're probably more widely read in theology than I am -- and I teach this stuff!"

"Theo, you know that I just fix water problems, flooded basements, and clogged toilets. I'm just a small fish in God's pond."

"John, you remind me of something said by John Gardner, who was the Secretary of Health, Education, and Welfare under President Lyndon Johnson. Gardner said, "The society which scorns excellence in plumbing as a humble activity and tolerates shoddiness in philosophy because it is an exalted activity will have neither good plumbing nor good philosophy: neither its pipes nor its theories will hold water."

Hornby and Ensel laughed and laughed at that quote, and for the next hour, they discussed the finer points of God's omnipresence, the state of believers who were already in heaven, and whether or not those saints paid attention to what was going on down here on earth. Neither was aware that their discussion was taking place in Aisle 7, Feminine Hygiene and Incontinence Aids.

 # Ch. 7

When Hornby got home, he opened the front door and called out, "Luther, I'm home! Got the dishes done from last night?"

He knew very well that the dirty dishes would still be in the sink and Luther would stumble out of the bedroom, leaving a warm, round indentation at the foot of Hornby's bed.

But Luther loved doing figure 8's around Hornby's legs and his deep purring was his way of saying, "I'm so glad you're home. Can we watch 'Columbo' tonight? And might we have an encore of that tv dinner which we enjoyed last night?"

As much as he appreciated Luther's company, Hornby really missed his long discussions with Ellie. They could talk about anything, often finishing each other's sentences. At their 50th wedding anniversary celebration, one of their friends described the Hornbys by saying, "Even their minds seem to be holding hands!"

Eleanor had had a distinguished career, first as a high school guidance counselor, then as head of the guidance department. She seemed to have that motherly or grandmotherly appearance that drew students with struggles to her like a magnet. Even though her primary job as a counselor was to help students select courses or make good decisions about which college to attend, much of her time was spent in listening to and providing wisdom to countless young men and women who needed "just a few minutes, Mrs. H?"

When she retired a year before her death, Mrs. Hornby had impacted literally thousands of young people on such critical issues as sexual purity; personality styles; parental respect; academic excellence; the pitfalls of popular culture; the importance of being an active member of a solid, local church; etc. After she left, the administration realized that it needed to hire two people to take her place: one as head of the guidance department and another as a confidante and counselor.

Her death left a lot of holes, and not just in my heart, thought Hornby, as he plopped into his recliner with Luther jumping up to lie next to him. "Luther," Hornby said out loud, "please don't take this the wrong way, but you're a pretty poor substitute for my Ellie. I'd sure love to have her back. If only I could have my wish . . ."

Luther perked up when he heard the word "wish." Hmmm. He thought to himself. "Wish" sounds like "fish" -- and I haven't had any tuna in a long time!

"Got you something special for dinner tonight," Hornby said to Luther. "It's that new Seven Seas Hungry Man Seafood Platter," he said. "Here -- it will take me just a few minutes to microwave it."

Luther licked his lips and thought, I'll bet we watch "Columbo" tonight. As long as I get the leftovers!

"I wonder what's on the 'Classics' TV channel?", Hornby asked as he took the dinner out of the microwave. "Doesn't that smell delicious, Luther?"

 # Ch. 8

Mrs. Scarlett O'Leary was Faithful Bible College's librarian -- and she took her job very seriously. Although she was always ready to help the students, especially in learning good research methods, she was a stickler for returning checked-out books on time. She would not hesitate to charge a student -- or a faculty member, for that matter -- ten cents per day for any books not returned when due.

One of her hobbies was collecting librarians' curses. Her favorite was from the monastery of San Pedro, Barcelona, which reads:

"For him that stealeth a book from this library, let it change into a serpent in his hand & rend him. Let him be struck with palsy, & all his members blasted. Let him languish in pain crying aloud for mercy, & let there be no surcease to his agony till he sink to dissolution. Let bookworms gnaw his entrails in token of the Worm that dieth not, & when at last he goeth to his final punishment, let the flames of hell consume him forever & aye."

She had several others framed and hung on her office wall. One was by Hugh, the abbot of Lobbes Abbey in Germany, who noticed in 1049 that a number of the monastery's books were missing. So he wrote on the last page of his catalogue:

"All those who do not books return
Are thieves, not borrowers, and earn
The punishment Justice demands;
Their sacrificial loss of hands,

May God, therefore, as witness see
That it be done unswervingly."

Two others were publicly displayed on Mrs. O'Leary's office wall. One was by a gentle Eleanor Worcester, who in 1440 wrote,

"This book is mine
And I it lost, and you it find,
I pray you heartily to be so kind,
That you will take a little pain,
To see my book brought home again."

With tongue-in-cheek, her absolute favorite curse was by the Parisian scribe Simon Vostre who completed a Book of Hours in 1502 with the lines

"Whoever steals this Book of Prayer
May he be ripped apart by swine,
His heart be splintered, this I swear,
And his body dragged along the Rhine."

Contrary to the impression these curses gave of Mrs. O'Leary's personality, she was nevertheless a sweet widow who had her sights set resolutely on none other than Dr. Theophilus Hornby. Mrs. O'Leary's husband had passed away about the same time as Mrs. Hornby, but she had finished her grieving her late husband's passing in record time.

Whenever Hornby came into the library, Mrs. O'Leary would drop what she was doing, would unceremoniously shove aside any student worker who dared to move toward assisting Dr. Hornby, and would whisper in her best, throaty, librarian voice, "Theo, how may I help you today?"

Hornby, although he was immensely observant in his Bible studies, was quite naive regarding Mrs. O'Leary's intentions. But the students knew, and did not hesitate to share with one another her latest efforts to turn Hornby's head her direction. Those students whose student work responsibilities put them on library detail would try to set up Dr. Hornby and Mrs. O'Leary by asking him some arcane question in class whose answer could only be found out by visiting FBC's stacks. And then the real observing would begin.

FBC had a monthly dessert get together at which the faculty could share about their recent writing projects or ministry opportunities, and, after appropriate cake or pie, the evening concluded with a time of prayer.

On this Friday evening Hornby had volunteered to read an original poem he had written while teaching his "Theological Methods and Issues" class.

The dean of the school, Dr. Sean Miller, opened the monthly meeting with prayer. "Tonight," he said, "we have as our special treat an original poem by our own Dr. Theophilus Hornby. Dr. Hornby."

The other faculty and staff clapped profusely, knowing that Hornby's contribution to the evening's festivities would be worth listening to.

"Friends," Hornby began, "as a few of you know, my 'Theological Methods and Issues' class can be a real challenge sometimes. Some students do unthinkable things to participles, like dangle them, and even maliciously split infinitives!"

The group laughed, but Hornby continued. "A few of our students think that research is stringing together a bunch of quotes from hard-to-understand experts, sometimes failing to cite the original sources. Very few of our charges intentionally plagiarize, but this situation inspired me to pen the following parody of a famous poem, entitled 'Footprints in the Sand."

The group all got quiet as they waited for Hornby to read his poem. "This poem is called 'Footnotes in the Surf.'"

He then read his poem:

FOOTNOTES IN THE SURF

One night I dreamed a dream

Of a research assignment — and I began to scheme

How to finish and get a great grade

But that wouldn't happen without some aid.

As I strolled on the beach thinking what I could do

It occurred to me that I could pursue

Not serious study but a quick treasure hunt

Into the works of others, an oft-used stunt

By lazy students who didn't care

Whose words they used, or ideas to share

Without attribution, without any guilt

And so I completed the research paper "I" built.

After turning it in and receiving it back

I was given an "A" — and that's a fact!

But then that night as I lay on my bed

I had a dream, a nightmare instead

And the Lord spoke to me what was undoubtedly true.

"My son — that's not your work. Others have carried you!"

"Oh, Theo. That was tremendous!", Mrs. O'Leary gushed as the meeting came to an end and everybody began heading home.

"You know, Theo, I happen to have some homemade apple cider and freshly-baked shortbread cookies waiting in my kitchen at home."

Mrs. O'Leary had heard that those two items were at the top of Hornby's list of most desirable comfort foods. But he was tired and said to Mrs. O'Leary, "Thank you, Mrs. O. But can I take a raincheck?"

"A raincheck? Theo -- you can call me Scarlett -- there's not a cloud in the sky. And you've already collected five rainchecks from me!"

At that precise moment in his personal history as a man, it dawned on Hornby -- could it possibly be -- that Mrs. O'Leary was hitting on him?! Man, he said to himself, have I been naive or what?

He stumbled on his words as he made his escape. "Mrs. O'Leary, I mean Scarlett, it just occurred to me that I have several books overdue that I had better turn in to the library tomorrow! I'll drop them off sometime in the morning."

"Oh, Theo. Don't worry about overdue books. I think you and I are a bit overdue, if you catch my meaning!"

Hornby could feel himself blushing as he grabbed his coat and jumped in his car.

When he got home, Luther climbed up on his lap, instinctively sensing something was upsetting Hornby. "Luther," Hornby said, "I sure miss my Ellie." Luther thought he said "jelly," and thought how good a jelly biscuit would be about right now.

Ch. 9

"I just love my 'calling'," John Smith said to himself. "I get to do God's work and fulfill my destiny!"

As he sat in his hotel room, Smith was thoroughly relishing the news reports of Delvaney's death. He thought to himself how much he enjoyed the hours of research and preparation — which were always followed by a perfect execution. He rehearsed his work out-loud as he reviewed the car "accident" he caused.

"First, I had to study *Vespula vulgaris*, otherwise known as the common wasp. I learned that the wasp's venom is as powerful as a rattlesnake's.

"I remember overhearing some of Delvaney's men in a bar talking about how their boss — a man feared by all — was deathly afraid of only one thing — wasps! His henchmen laughed as they remembered how he had jumped straight up at a family meeting when he thought a wasp was flying near his head. He explained his action by telling the story of when, as a child on his tenth birthday, he had had a wasp nest fall behind his sweatshirt as he climbed his favorite tree. He had gotten stung about 25 times and almost died.

"I love it!", Smith said. "Delvaney didn't get stung even once this time!" Smith gushed as he recalled the medical examiner's findings. "Just the thought of a wasp in his car was enough to do him in!" Smith laughed out loud as he reflected on his perfect plan.

He had read up on wasps and learned that a captured wasp could be put to sleep with just a small amount of carbon dioxide. "And when Delvaney opened that small box with the card on top saying 'Congratulations!', he didn't realize that the chocolate truffles were hiding a sleeping wasp! Shortly after the box was opened, the air woke up the wasp and the rest is, as they say, blessed history!"

Smith picked up his Bible and began to read some of his favorite passages. He read verses from Numbers 35 about a man appointed by God.

As he read, Smith reviewed the details of "the avenger of blood." God decreed that six Levite cities were to be "cities of refuge" to which a killer of someone might flee and await trial before the assembly. If that person had committed murder (striking a person with something made out of iron, stone, or wood), "the avenger of blood shall put the murderer to death; when the avenger comes upon the murderer, the avenger shall put the murderer to death" (Num. 35:19). God also commanded execution by the avenger for someone who out of enmity hits another with their fist and they die.

However, Smith continued to read, the avenger of blood can't execute someone who pushes another or throws something at them unintentionally or, without seeing them, drops a stone on them, and they die. No harm was intended and, after a trial before the assembly, the accused must go back to the city of refuge and stay there until the death of the high priest.

Smith finished his reading of Numbers 35 by noting that if the accused ever goes outside the limits of the city of refuge to which they fled and the avenger of blood finds them outside the city, the avenger of blood may kill the accused without being guilty of murder.

"I prefer my work to be quiet and private, unlike the Old Testament's avenger of blood," Smith said to himself. "I wonder what my next assignment might be."

Ch. 10

"Where the hell am I - and how did I get here?", Bubba Delvaney said out loud. "It's pitch black in this place and I have never smelled such a putrid stench in my life!"

"What do I remember? Oh, yeah, I heard that dreadful sound as I was driving away from the party and I think — could it possibly be? — I think I drove off a cliff! So why am I still alive? Or am I?"

Ch. 11

"Intro to Theology 101" was one of Hornby's favorite classes to teach. It gave him a chance to survey the ten major areas of Christian doctrine and, hopefully, to whet the appetite of his students to all things theological.

"Today, students," Dr. Hornby said, "we're going to deal with a very difficult subject. The subject is what happens to those who die without a saving knowledge of Jesus."

"Dr. Hornby?" one young lady raised her hand. "Are you talking about . . ." (she blushed when she said the next word) ". . . hell?"

"Yes, as a matter of fact, I am." Hornby could see on the 30 or so students in the class that he had their undivided attention. "Many people who claim to be Christians have abandoned the idea of eternal, conscious punishment, but I hope to show that the Bible actually teaches that 'the wicked' — those who die without Christ — will be separated from God and His people forever and will undergo everlasting punishment."

"But my pastor taught us that all will eventually get to heaven!" one student in the back said. "In fact, he said that God is too loving to send anyone to hell and man isn't sinful enough to merit eternal punishment."

"That's a very common view," Dr. Hornby replied. "It's usually called universalism, but it's not what the Bible teaches." Hornby went on to show several clear Scriptures which indicated that there will be a final separation of those in Christ from those who did not trust Him as their Savior.

"I've had some Seventh-Day Adventist friends who told me that those who die without Christ will eventually be annihilated, put out of existence, by God," another student stated. "In fact, they told me that God shouldn't be seen as a cosmic torturer!"

"That's a view known as conditionalism or annihilationism," Hornby said. "In fact, one of the best known Evangelical leaders, John R.W. Stott, was a conditionalist. But, again, that's not what the Bible teaches. Hornby pointed out a number of Scriptures which indicated that "the wicked" will undergo eternal, conscious punishment.

"Perhaps there will be numerous opportunities to trust Christ after death?", asked a student named Michael Delganey. "Must we really believe that God's grace toward the lost will end at death? Didn't Jesus preach to the dead when He descended to hell between His death and His resurrection?"

Hornby thought for a moment. "You've asked a great question. Michael, is it? Some have thought that Christ's so-called descent into hell is explained to us in I Peter 3. This view is sometimes called 'the post-mortem conversion' view." Hornby went on to show that I Peter 3 is really talking about Jesus preaching through Noah to the unbelievers of Noah's day. And that Jesus did not offer a second or third or fourth chance for salvation to people after their deaths.

"But, Dr. Hornby," Michael responded. "Do you really believe that those who die without believing in Jesus will be eternally condemned and never, ever have a chance to get right with God? Really?"

Hornby could see that Michael's question was more than merely academic. "I believe that we should grieve for those who have died without Christ, but for them it is too late. That's why the Bible puts such an emphasis on sharing our faith with people now. On earth. Before they die."

Michael's head was down on his desk. After Hornby finished his lecture, the class ended — he assigned twenty Scriptures for the students to look up for their next session of Intro to Theology. He then went over to Michael to talk with him.

"Michael," Dr. Hornby said, "I know this is a disturbing topic. Could there even be a more disturbing topic than this one? Are you thinking about someone you care about who has died without trusting Jesus?"

Michael's eyes filled with tears. "Yes, Dr. Hornby! My uncle. I don't have any reason to believe that he died believing in Jesus! And now he is lost . . . forever!"

Hornby pulled up a desk next to Michael and wished he had his Ellie with him. She would know what to do. She would put her arm around Michael and just let him cry. All Hornby could do was ask him, "Would you want to tell me a bit about your uncle, Michael?"

"Well, sir, you need to know that my last name was changed a couple of years ago."

"Changed?" Dr. Hornby responded.

"Yessir. Our last name used to be 'Delvaney.' My father changed our last name because of the criminal mob Delvaney. My uncle was Bubba Delvaney who died last year in a car accident."

Ch. 12

Faithful Bible College's cafeteria would never make the cover of Martha Stewart's "The 50 Most Attractive College Dining Halls in the States," but the area was neat and comfortable and the meals prepared by Sissie Borden were delicious. Students often had to be asked to leave the cafeteria when it was closing because they could have seconds or thirds and the atmosphere was perfect for meeting in small groups and talking about their classes.

The other perk in the dining hall was that there was no separate faculty dining area. The teachers at FBC would eat with the students to discuss course assignments, questions about life, or just to shoot the breeze. On every annual review of FBC's facilities students always gave the highest marks to Miss Borden's menus and especially the faculty regularly being available for conversation.

Although most of the tables were designed to seat 6-8 diners, there was several smaller tables in the corners of the dining hall for more private conversations.

Hornby entered the cafeteria and immediately noticed Michael Delganey sitting by himself at one of the smaller tables. "Mind if I join you?", Hornby asked.

"Of course, Professor Hornby. I'd be honored!" Michael stood up as Hornby took his seat.

"Michael," Dr. Hornby said, "do you mind telling me a bit more about your family and your background?"

"Well, sir, it's kind of complicated. My family is originally from the Chicago area, but we moved away years ago."

"Why did your family move away from Chicago?", Hornby asked.

"It's a bit embarrassing, but it was well known that the Delvaney family (that was our last name before . . . well, I believe I shared that with you already) were, shall we say, major players in the criminal world of Chicago. My father had nothing to do with his brother or his cousins. In fact, my Dad had shared the gospel with each of them — and was scoffed at for believing 'all that stuff.'"

"Did you lose all contact with your family when you moved away?", Hornby asked.

"Pretty much. I told you a bit about my favorite uncle. We called him 'Uncle Bubba.' He was a huge man, but very gentle and friendly. When I was small he gave me horsey-back rides when he came to visit."

"This is the Uncle Bubba who died?"

Michael's eyes filled with tears. "Yes, he passed away about a year ago. I miss him terribly. He used to take me for a ride in his beautiful Lexus."

Hornby cautiously said, "Do you mind telling me how he died, Michael?"

"Well, sir, he was being charged with some very serious crimes. There were rumors that some key witnesses had gone missing. It appears that after celebrating being found innocent in court, he just drove off a cliff!"

"Drove off a cliff? Why would he do such a thing?"

Michael looked down. "I don't know, Sir. The police have no explanation. There was no evidence that another car was involved or that he skidded to avoid a deer or anything like that. And I know my uncle. He would not have committed suicide!"

"Michael, I'm so sorry for your loss," Hornby said.

"But, Dr. Hornby, that's not the worst of it!"

"What do you mean, Michael?"

"I mean, if my uncle died without a saving knowledge of Jesus Christ, he is lost forever!" Michael burst into tears, not caring if any other students saw him crying in the cafeteria.

Hornby tried to comfort Michael, but felt quite inept in his attempt. "Michael, I will be praying that the Lord will give you comfort. Please drop by my office anytime that you want to talk."

"I will, Sir. And thank you for listening."

As Hornby left the cafeteria, he thought to himself, I wonder why more of us don't have that kind of love for those we care about who die without being in Jesus. Hornby also thought about how he would really like to find out why Bubba drove over that cliff.

 # Ch. 13

"You know, there's a lot of verses about the sins of the fathers being visited upon their children," John Smith said to himself out loud. "I would imagine that such Scriptures apply also to brothers, right?"

Taking out Bubba Delvaney was important, Smith thought to himself. But what other family members merit my expertise? He asked himself, "I think that Bubba had a brother, right? I wonder where I might find him?"

Ch. 14

Henry Delganey was so proud of his son Michael. It had taken Michael a while to adjust to the move from Chicago, and he had seemed reluctant to start making friends.

But Henry and his wife Miriam had settled into a comfortable life near Faithful Bible College. They had been able to purchase a nice mountain cabin about twenty miles from the campus.

Miriam said, "Henry, is Michael doing okay with his studies? Any idea how he's liking the dorm? Is he making any new friends? He really could do a better job keeping in touch with his mother!"

"Michael has texted me a couple of times. He's still quite upset about his uncle's death. But he's told me some about his classes. His favorite professor is a Dr. Hornby. What a strange name!"

Miriam replied, "I just looked up that name on the internet and there was a famous Frank Hornby who was an English inventor back in the early twentieth century. He actually used his mechanical skills to create toys like the system called 'Meccano.' And he made a fortune from his model railways and the brand 'Dinky Toys.'"

"Well, I don't know if this Dr. Hornby is related to that toy guy or not," Henry said. "I'm just glad Michael is enjoying his studies. Perhaps they will help him come to terms with our move — and the loss of his beloved uncle."

"'Beloved uncle?!," Miriam said. "He was a criminal. And I'm glad we got out of Chicago!"

"Of course you are right, Dear. And I really don't know how much Michael knows about Uncle Bubba. You and I have prayed for that side of the family for years. And we specifically prayed for Bubba's salvation after I had that long talk with him two Christmases ago."

Miriam said, "Did Bubba really call you a 'religious wimp'?"

"I'm afraid so, Dear. I just pray that he got right with the Lord before, you know, his accident." Henry looked at a photograph of Michael when he was eight and Uncle Bubba with Michael on his back.

Miriam put her arm around her husband. "You tried, Honey, to reach Bubba with the gospel. But I guess he was too blinded by the money he was making with that side of the family."

Ch. 15

Tuesday morning's class was one of Hornby's favorites. In reality, all of his classes were his favorites, for he considered shaping young minds an incredible privilege.

"Theological Methods and Issues" was an upper-level research class in which students learned how to investigate an issue and write persuasive, evidence-based papers on their chosen topic. And the topics were quite varied. Some chose to take on the issue of abortion and cultural values. Others worked on the topic of male leadership in the Scriptures. And still others investigated unusual subjects that they had thought about for a long time.

Hornby saw his job as helping the student sharpen his or her research question, pursue the best sources for information, and respond to the issue in a culturally relevant manner. Each year as he taught this particular course, he was impressed with the excellent work of most of the students. In fact, last year he had self-published the top ten papers in the class as a book entitled "Thinking about Theology." It had become a best seller — among the students' parents and relatives!

But not all his students were eager to receive his wisdom in sharpening and researching their papers. One older female student proposed writing her paper on the Gullah people of South Carolina. Dr. Hornby, who knew a bit about that Low Country people group, suggested several ways in which that topic could be a bit more focused.

"I remember that conversation as if it were yesterday," Hornby said out loud to himself. "My student listened to my ideas, then looked at me and said, 'If I followed your advice, Dr. Hornby, that would be your paper, not mine!'" Oh, well, he thought to himself. You can't help everyone.

Hornby prided himself on his ability to find — and fix — every grammatical error in a student's paper. He not only dealt with dangling participles and split infinitives, but simple matters such as punctuation errors, comma splices, and unclear antecedents. He thought back on an email he received from one student who was considering taking his "Theological Methods and Issues" class. He wrote the student, welcoming her into the class, and added that he was death on grammatical errors and she should be prepared to proof-read her final paper several times.

He got back the following email: "Dr. Hornby, I read what you said about your correcting grammar mistakes, and I want you to know that you hurt my feeling."

Hornby didn't know how to respond. He wanted to write, "I'm sorry you were offended, and I believe you wanted to say 'you hurt my feelings', but I will do my best to help you compose the best paper you can." Instead he left out the correction and assured her he was looking forward to working with her.

Some students thought that the FBC faculty did not carefully read student papers, but just skimmed them and assigned grades. "Ha!", Hornby laughed to himself, as he recalled reading a rather lengthy paper on "The Mystics of the Middle Ages" by Kathy, an excellent student in his class. In the middle of her discussion of the philosophical foundation of mysticism, she wrote in a small footnote, "Dr. Hornby, if you are reading this whole paper, I will buy you a Burger King Whooper Meal Friday night at midnight!"

She and her friends were shocked to see Hornby enter the local Burger King at 11:59 pm on Friday night wearing a Burger King crown with a Burger King napkin tucked into his dress shirt and carrying a fork and a knife! That was one delicious meal, Hornby thought to himself!

Ch. 16

"There is no accountability today!", John Smith said out loud to himself. He was watching the evening news and its report of another school shooting. "There needs to be justice! Sin must be punished! Evil must be confronted!"

As he had his morning devotions, Smith gravitated to his favorite verses about God being an avenging God, a wrathful God, a God who cannot overlook sin.

"We have no 'cities of refuge today,'" he said to himself. "So there's no possibility of those who deserve wrath to hide themselves and wait for a trial. And that's where I come in!" Smith smiled to himself as he began his plans of meting out God's righteous punishment on wrong- doers.

He reread the obituary for Bubba Delvaney, noticing that there was one brother who was living somewhere in North Carolina. "I just may have to pay him a little visit," Smith said as he packed a small travel bag. "It is," he said, "a 'fearful thing to fall into the hands of the living God,'" quoting one of his best-loved verses from the King James' version of Hebrews 10. "It's also a fearful thing to fall . . . into my hands!"

Ch. 17

Officer Bondo had been with the Chicago/Fayetteville Police Department for five years. And he so wanted to become a detective. Writing parking tickets and chasing drugged teenagers was not his idea of serious police work.

"We've closed the book on the Delvaney accident, Bondo," said Sargent Sanders as he slapped the file down on his desk. "I guess we'll never know why he drove off that cliff!"

Well, that conclusion just doesn't work with me, Bondo thought to himself. He picked up the file to take it to the cold case locker, but first he stepped into the copy room to make a copy for himself. "I'm going to make detective, if it's the last thing I do!"

Bondo drove home after his shift and began laying out his plan. "I haven't had Italian in quite a while," he said out loud. As he set his GPS for Pontefiori's Family Restaurant, he thought to himself, What are you getting into, Bondo? You just gonna grab a seat next to the crime family and pepper them with questions?! "Yes," he said to himself. "That's exactly what I'm going to do!"

He waited until about 8 pm. He had heard that the members of Bubba's family gathered at Mama Pontefiori's on Thursday evenings to report on their "businesses" and just to spend some time together.

When Bondo walked in he was not in uniform. He walked right up to the family table and pulled out a chair. "Hey, Buster, what do you think you're doin'?" said Fernando, Bubba's bodyguard.

"Calm down, my friend," Bondo said. "I'm not here to make trouble."

"Hey, he's a cop from around here. What you want, Copper?", said another rather large, muscled family member.

"I'm only here to ask a few questions. Our investigation of Mr. Delvaney's accident gave us no answers why he would simply drive off that cliff."

"No kidding, Einstein! What do you think you can do about it? You're just a beat cop. You're not even a detective!" This was said by Paschal, one of the older members of the family.

"You need to know that I don't take delight in the death of anyone," Bondo said. "But it bugs the heck out of me that my police department has given up finding some answers. That's all I want."

"Sure, Officer, uh . . .?" Fernando asked.

"Bondo. Alex Bondo. I may not be a detective. Yet. But I'd like your cooperation in my off-the-books investigation. What do you have to lose?"

"Lose? We don't want no cop snooping around our business. Get lost, my man!" Paschal growled.

"Listen. My mamma always said I was stubborn. And I'm going to pursue this. Either with or without your help!" He swallowed hard, surprised at his own brashness.

"What do you need to know, Officer Bondo?" Fernando sat down and faced him. "We want to know what happened as well."

He began with his list of questions about possible enemies, run-ins with competitors, angry family members. To each of his queries the family gave their best, but guarded, answers.

As he was about to leave, Bondo thanked the family and said he would do his best to get some answers. He hesitated as he thought about the last question he was going to ask. "But," he said to himself, "this is no time to be timid."

He turned to look at the table of Bubba's friends and family and said, "I don't know how to ask this, but was there anyone or anything that Mr. Delvaney was afraid of?"

Fernando let out an angry, "What?! That man was not afraid of anything! And how dare you imply that he was?"

Bondo almost feared getting slugged by the beefy bodyguard, but he quietly left the restaurant. As he was opening his car door, he heard someone say, "Officer Bondo?"

"Yes?"

Paschal stepped into the street light. "I really want to find out what happened to Bubba and it may sound crazy, but there was only one thing that I can think of that terrified Bubba."

"And what would that have been?", Bondo asked.

"He was afraid of . . . wasps. He would jump sky high if there was a wasp in the room. In fact, a few of us were laughing about that at Mike's Tavern the other week. Just thought you'd want to know."

"Thanks, Paschal," Bondo said. As he drove away from the restaurant, he noticed that his brake pedal was a bit mushy. "I'd better get my brakes checked at the motor pool this week!" But that opportunity would not, unfortunately, present itself.

Ch. 18

"Who's in charge here?", growled Sargent Sanders. "Where's my Officer Bondo?"

Sanders gripped the ER nurses' station, leaning over to bark at the thin, blond young woman who was filling in charts.

"Sir, I'm afraid Officer Bondo is in the ICU. Only family members are allowed to see him."

"I AM family, Miss Hunter!" Sanders looked like he was going to jump over the desk when the attending ER physician came around the corner. "What's happening here?", he asked.

"I'm Officer Bondo's boss — and I want to see him right now!"

"I'm afraid that's impossible, Sargent. He's in a coma."

"A coma? What in the world happened to him? His wife called me and told me he was taken to the hospital."

"I'm not sure what happened, but he crashed his patrol car into a patch of birch trees off Highway 77."

"Highway 77? That's way out of our jurisdiction. And nowhere near Bondo's home."

"Well, all I can tell you is that he will survive. He's got two broken legs, a ruptured spleen, and a pretty severe concussion. If it hadn't been for the patrol car's airbags and the patient's excellent physical condition, I don't think he would have made it."

"Doc, please call me when he wakes up. He's young, but he's an excellent driver. I need to know what happened to him."

"Will do, Sargent Sanders. Now, if you will excuse me, I've got some other patients to attend to."

As Sanders started to leave, he turned around and said to the young nurse, "I apologize for my abruptness, Miss. Please do all you can for my Officer."

"You can count on it, Sir."

John Smith was sitting close by in the patients' section of the ER and was overhearing most of the conversations. "I hope this accident will discourage Bondo from doing any more investigating." He said to himself as he walked to his car. "I don't really have any desire to finish off this cop."

Ch. 19

Wednesday morning was one of Hornby's most anticipated classes. He had taught "Eternal Destinies" as an upper-level theology course for several years, and, although only five seniors had signed up for it this semester, he was pleased with their enthusiasm.

With the Dean's permission, Hornby invited leaders of several cults to come to his class and lecture on the topic of the end times from their perspectives. As he lined up his guests, he gave each of them a brief overview of the course and the kind of Evangelical students they would be speaking to.

For the next eight weeks Hornby scheduled 30 minute lectures by such guests as: the head of the Jehovah's Witnesses in the state, a female orthodox rabbi, two Christian Science ladies, a couple of Mormon elders from the neighborhood, a Buddhist priest, and a chiropractor who represented the Baha'i religion.

"I hope this year's class will be as courteous as previous years," Hornby said to himself. Those former students had conducted themselves admirably as they listened, took notes, and asked questions of the guest speakers from the various cults and religions.

Hornby's students had been trained well for they usually asked two probing questions of each of the guests after their lectures were finished: (1) What is your final authority for what you believe? and (2) What is your perspective on the Person and Work of Jesus Christ?

I'm sure this semester's class will be just as polite — and perceptive — Hornby thought to himself. He remembered a previous year when the leader of the local Jehovah's Witnesses Kingdom Hall gave his guest lecture. The students had challenged him on his dismissal of the biblical truth of eternal hell and had pretty much bested him on the topic of Jesus' deity.

After the class was over, Hornby made it his practice to walk the guest lecturer to his or her car, giving them a small gift of appreciation for their lecture. He also took the opportunity to share the gospel as best he could.

He remembered talking with Mike, the Jehovah's Witness leader, about the gospel. Mike was dressed in a three-piece suit and was doing his best to leave the campus as soon as he could. After he accepted Hornby's small gift, Mike began jumping up and down and slapping at his legs! This was unusual behavior for a Jehovah's Witness. It turned out that Mike had been standing on a red ant hill and was being bitten by a kazillion fire ants! It was all Hornby could do to keep himself from saying, "You know, Mike, bad doctrine sometimes brings bad consequences!" But Hornby simply waved goodbye as Mike hurriedly drove off.

Bad doctrine does bring bad consequences, Hornby thought to himself, as he got ready to lecture to his "Eternal Destiny" students. And what worse consequence could there be than eternal hell?

Ch. 20

"I have never felt such abandonment in my life!", Bubba said to himself. "Where am I? Am I in a coma from the accident? There's this searing pain throughout my body. Why aren't they giving me drugs?"

As he tried to look around Bubba became acutely aware that he was in a dark place. Not a dark place like one's closet or out in the woods camping. No. A darkness like being in the bowels of a damp underground cavern.

He remembered hearing a Sunday School lesson when he was a young boy about a darkness that "could be felt" which God inflicted on the Egyptians as He prepared to free His people from slavery. "I can almost touch this darkness," Bubba said. His own voice sounded odd, ethereal, distorted, as if he were stuck in some deserted, isolated pit.

"Sunday School!, that was a joke! What a bunch of nonsense that whole church thing was! What a waste of time!" Bubba's pain seemed to be increasing. He reached his right hand to touch his side and his side felt really strange, almost numb. "How am I ever going to get out of this place?", he cried out in the darkness.

Ch. 21

"How's it going, Son?" Henry Delganey asked over the phone. "Classes going well?"

"They're going great, Dad," Michael said. "I've made a few friends. I'm getting really challenged to do my best in my studies."

"That's wonderful, Michael. What are the teachers like?"

"Dad, that's one of the best parts of being here at FBC. The faculty really care about us students."

"Good to hear, Michael," said his father. "So it's not just a lot of boring lectures and endless home-work assignments?"

"There's plenty of work to do, that's for sure. But I'm talking about the teachers' making them-selves available for the students."

Henry squeezed Miriam's hand as they were listening to their son on their cell phone's speaker. "Have you had any serious personal conversations with any of the faculty?" Henry and Miriam were concerned with Michael's grief over the loss of his uncle.

"Yes, as a matter of fact, I have. My favorite prof is a Dr. Theophilus Hornby. He teaches bibli-cal studies."

"Really?", asked Michael's mom. "But he's spent some time with you?"

"That's the great thing about it, Mom. We were talking in class about the after-life and what hap-pens when people die without Jesus. And, well, Dr. Hornby pretty much laid in on the line."

"What do you mean, Son?", Henry asked.

"Dr. Hornby really knows the Scriptures and he showed us the awful truth that those who die without Christ are lost forever."

"What happened then, Michael?"

"Well, Dr. Hornby could see that I was upset and approached me after class — and even had lunch with me the next day — to help me with my questions."

"You're referring to Uncle Bubba's passing, right?" Henry and Miriam had been praying every morning that Michael would find peace about that tragedy.

"Yes. And he sympathized with my sadness. But he didn't water down or compromise the Bible's teaching about eternal lostness. He did ask me a few questions about the accident."

"Really?", responded both parents in unison.

"And you know what I think? I think he's going to do a bit of looking into Uncle Bubba's car accident for himself."

****

"It's amazing how easy it is to wiretap someone's phone," John Smith said to himself. He had been listening to every word of their conversation. "Hornby, huh? I guess I'll just have to look up this Hornby character."

Ch. 22

Monday morning's "Theology 101" class was one of Hornby's most enjoyable. Because the students were freshmen, their questions created great discussions, sometimes generating debates between various perspectives.

"Debates are good," Hornby said as he closed his office door and began walking toward the classroom. "I really want my students to think for themselves." He remembered G.K. Chesterton's statement in defense of good argumentation: "What good are words," Chesterton asked, "if you can't argue over them?"

Hornby especially appreciated the beginning few minutes of class, a segment his students also looked forward to. It was his practice to share a short devotional from the Bible in every one of his sessions, and today was no exception. He had been working his way through John 11, the story of the raising of Lazarus. Hornby had entitled this little series "Friends Don't Let Friends . . . Die!" "But that's exactly what Jesus did with His friend Lazarus, right, students?"

Hornby's short devotional was followed by a vigorous discussion of God's allowing — sometimes arranging — difficult circumstances in our lives for His glory.

After a brief word of prayer, Hornby said, "This morning, class, we're going to talk about a subject that is very much related to our present discussion about the death — and subsequent resurrection —

of Jesus' friend Lazarus. The topic is the sovereignty of God."

"But, Dr. Hornby, isn't that a topic that pretty much divides Christians from one another?", asked a young coed on the front row.

"Yes, I'm afraid so. Typically the topic of God's sovereignty has divided believers into two categories: those who emphasize man's free will (the Arminians) and those who put their emphasis on God's control (the Calvinists)."

"Which category do you fit in, Dr. Hornby?", asked Michael Delganey, obviously intrigued by the topic.

"Great question, Michael. But in some ways not a very easy one to answer."

"How do you mean, Sir?"

"Well, above all I want to be biblical in my theology. And the challenge in this area is that there is biblical data on both sides of the debate."

"What would be some of the data on the Armenian side?", asked a student in the back.

"Great question," Hornby said. "And I hope you won't be offended, but the term you want is 'Arminian', not 'Armenian.' Armenians are those who come from the country of Armenia, a former Soviet republic in Asia. I guess you could have an Arminian Armenian, couldn't you?"

The class laughed, including the student who confused the two terms.

"But back to your question. We get several Scriptures that emphasize man's free will (the Arminian perspective) such as Mark 8's statement about 'whosoever will come after me' and Joshua's famous challenge in Joshua 24 to 'choose you this day whom you will serve.' The Bible is filled with expressions that imply man has the power to choose or not choose the Lord. In fact, Jesus says in Matthew 23, 'O Jerusalem, Jerusalem, thou that killest the prophets, and stonest them which are sent unto thee, how often would I have gathered thy children together, even as a hen gathereth her chickens under her wings, and ye would not!' I'm quoting the King James' version. It just sounds better! Such statements certainly seem to imply man's free will, don't you think?"

Hornby could see the students' thinking hard.

"But, Dr. Hornby, what's the evidence for the other side, the sovereignty of God side?", asked an older student.

"Well, we do get verses about predestination, such as Romans 8 which says, 'For whom he did foreknow, he also did predestinate to be conformed to the image of his Son, that he might be the first-born among many brethren.'

"And we also get some challenging statements like Acts 13 which tells about the Gentiles who heard Paul and Barnabas share the gospel: 'And when the Gentiles heard this, they were glad, and glorified the word of the Lord: and as many as were ordained to eternal life believed.' 'Ordained to eternal life' — hmmm," Hornby said.

"So God sovereignly chooses who will believe in Jesus?!", asked a tall, lanky young man.

Hornby thought for a moment. "We need to be careful not to overstate our position. I once heard a Bible college president (not ours here at FBC) say that our challenge is to "remain in the center of biblical tension."

"What in the world does that mean, Dr. Horn-by?", asked the same student.

"It means that our theological perspective, our theological framework, should not have power over what the Bible actually says. We don't determine what the Bible says and what it means by our theology. We should derive our theology from what Scripture teaches."

"So, I believe there is truth in both the Arminian and the Calvinist views. For the Arminian, the emphasis is on responding to the gospel. For the Calvinist, the emphasis is on God's electing those who will believe. The danger for the Arminian is that it can fairly quickly become a kind of works-salvation. The danger for the Calvinist is that it can degenerate into a kind of fatalism (God knows who will believe and there's nothing for us to do)."

"So, what's the answer, Professor?", asked a female student who was sitting at the back of the classroom.

"The answer, I would suggest, is to take all of the Word of God seriously, allowing every text to make its point, and not try to force any verses into our preconceived notions. The answer is that the gospel must be proclaimed and believed. And God will bless our efforts — both here and in other countries — to be faithful in our evangelism and missions."

"There are other issues that are impacted by the Arminian/Calvinist debate," Dr. Hornby said. "Such as the question, 'Can one lose his salvation?'"

"The broader topic — God's sovereignty — has very practical implications, students. It means, for example, that nothing in this life is accidental.

God either ordains all things or allows all things. The biblical perspective is that He actively ordains some things and He, in a sense, passively allows other things. So human beings have, at least to some degree, free will or choice."

Michael Delganey thought to himself. No accidents, huh? So what happened to my Uncle Bubba?

Hornby did not miss the pensive look on Michael's face and decided then and there that he would do a bit of investigating that critical event in his student's life.

Do I really believe that there are no accidents in life?, Hornby thought to himself. God uses human agents to fulfill His purposes. Human beings make choices. And their choices impact — sometimes catastrophically — the lives of others.

He was thinking about his student Michael who had lost his uncle to a car accident. I wonder if I could get access to the police report?, Hornby asked.

The next day Hornby called the Chicago/Fayetteville Police Department and his call was directed to Sargent Sanders.

"Yes, sir, can I help you?" Sanders said.

"Well, Sargent, I'm Dr. Hornby, a teacher at Faithful Bible College and I'm concerned about one of my students."

"What seems to be the problem, Dr. Hornby?"

"My student is Michael Delganey and his uncle Bubba Delvaney died in a car accident last year. I'm just wondering if I could get a look at the police report?"

"Why would you want to see the report, Professor?"

"I'm just concerned about my student. Was the cause of the accident determined?"

"No, unfortunately," Sanders said with what appeared to be a bit of embarrassment. "It looks like he just drove off the cliff. And there's no evidence that he was considering suicide. So, we've had to close the case. But I have no problem with your looking over the report."

"That's great, Sargent. Would I be able to talk to the investigating officer?"

"Of course. But you might get more details from one of our deputies who wants to become a detective. Although that might be a bit of a challenge."

"Why's that, Sargent Sanders?" Hornby asked.

"Well, Officer Bondo is still in the hospital recovering from his own car accident."

"I'm sorry to hear that. When did his car accident take place?"

"Oh, about a month after we had closed the Delvaney investigation. I'd be glad to give you Bondo's room number at Bethesda Hospital."

Sanders asked his secretary to make a copy of the police report and email it to Hornby. Hornby thanked the Sargent and hung up the phone.

After he received and reviewed the police report, Hornby got in his car and drove to Bethesda Hospital. He stopped at the nurses' desk in the critical care unit and asked to see Officer Bondo.

"He might be sleeping, uh, Dr. Hornby was it?" "Yes. I appreciate your help."

"You can go in, Sir," the nurse said. "He is awake and just finished his lunch."

Hornby entered Bondo's hospital room, hoping he could get some answers to his questions. He did not notice the large man sitting in the visitor's lounge just across from Bondo's room.

"Looks like we have another actor in this little drama," John Smith said to himself. "This is getting a bit more complicated than I had hoped."

"Officer Bondo?", Hornby asked as he lightly tapped on the hospital door.

"Yes?", came a weak, strained voice.

"Officer Bondo, my name is Theophilus Hornby and I'm a teacher at Faithful Bible College. I wonder if I could speak with you for a few minutes?"

Bondo struggled to sit a bit upright. His two legs were in casts and he looked pale and exhausted.

"I promise not to take too much of your time," Hornby said.

"How can I help you, is it Dr. Hornby?"

"Please call me Theo. All my friends do. I am so sorry about your car accident. Would you mind if I prayed for you after our conversation?" Hornby had never had anyone refuse his invitation to pray for them.

Bondo smiled. "I would appreciate your praying for me. I'm doing better, but I'll take all the prayers I can get! What did you want to talk about?"

Hornby explained a bit about his concern for his student Michael whose Uncle Bubba was killed in a car accident. "I understand you were doing a bit of investigative work on that accident?"

"Yes, until I had my accident. I still don't know how I lost my brakes. There was nothing that I could do!"

Hornby's eyes showed a deep concern for Bondo and his almost losing his life. "Were you able to find out any information about Delvaney's accident? I understand the inquiry is officially closed?"

"Yes, and I'm not at all happy about that! In fact, I went to the Delvaney family's favorite restaurant to ask my questions."

"Really? That took some courage! Michael, my student, told me that they are reputed to be major players in the Chicago crime world. In fact, his family changed their last name to Delganey to distance themselves from those relatives."

"I did not know that," Bondo said. "After some initial hesitation, the family talked to me and actually wished me well in trying to find out why Bubba would simply drive off a cliff."

"Were you able to gather any new information in meeting with them?", Hornby could see that Bondo was getting tired, so he started to conclude their conversation.

"It's the strangest thing. One of the family members met me at my car and said that there was only one thing that Bubba feared in life."

"What did he say that was?"

"He said that Bubba had a deathly fear of . . . wasps!"

"Really? What happened then?"

"I thanked him for talking with me — and then I got in my car, noticed the brakes were quite loose, and crashed into some trees."

"Officer Bondo, I'm so glad the Lord spared your life!"

"Me too! I'm not ready to meet my Maker just yet!"

"I really appreciate your time and I will pray for your full recovery. And just so you know, I'm not just a professor of theology. I'm also a kind of pastor. And I love to talk to people about the often-avoided topic of getting ready to meet their Maker!"

With those words, Hornby laid his hand on Bondo's shoulder and prayed for him.

"Thank you again for meeting with me, Officer. Mind if I drop by again to check up on you?"

Bondo smiled a weary smile. "Not at all. And God bless you as you try to help Michael."

Ch. 25

"Anyone there?" Bubba screamed, but no one answered. He felt that he was completely alone.

"I must be in a coma. And this must be a dream." He reached down with his hand and pinched his leg. "Ow! That hurt! And it felt like a hot iron. This is no dream! How do I get outta here?"

Ch. 26

Mrs. Scarlett O'Leary arrived at FBC's library at 7:30 am as was her custom. "That's odd," she said. "The front door to the library is open. And there are some lights on in the reference section."

As she entered the lobby of the library, she could see a large man standing, looking at some weighty tomes.

"Excuse me," she said. "How did you get into the library?"

John Smith looked at her, not at all surprised that he was no longer alone. He had piercing brown eyes and his face seemed to show no emotion or expression.

"I'm so sorry, but the night watchman let me in. He said you'd be along in a few minutes. I only needed to do some research. I hope you'll forgive me being in such a hurry." John Smith closed the reference book he had on the table and started to put it back on the shelf.

"That's okay, Mr., uh . . .?"

"My name is Smith. John Smith. I know. I know. Can one have a more common name?" Smith smiled, but it seemed forced and almost mechanical.

"It's just that FBC's library is for students and faculty only. You'll need a day pass if you wish to do research here. And, please don't re-shelve that reference book you were using. I'll be glad to do that for you. You know, students are always putting books back, often in the wrong spot, and they sometimes are lost forever."

Mrs. O'Leary moved to her desk behind the check-out counter as she said this. She couldn't stifle a small gasp as she watched Smith stand up. He looked to be over six feet tall and probably weighed over three hundred pounds.

"Of course, I understand, Mrs. O'Leary," Smith said, noticing her name plate on her desk. "If you don't mind I'll apply for a guest pass the next time I'm here."

Mrs. O'Leary watched Smith gather his backpack and head for the library's front door.

"Would you mind if I ask you a question, Mrs. O'Leary?" Smith used his right arm to gesture toward her.

"No, of course not. That's why I'm here. You know, we librarians love questions!"

Smith looked at Mrs. O'Leary with what appeared to be a penetrating, almost diabolical, gaze. "Do you happen to know if Dr. Hornby is in today? I was hoping to meet up with him a little later."

A very slight blush made its way from Mrs. O'Leary's neck up to her face as she thought about Theo and how much she wanted a relationship with him.

"I'm sorry, but I don't know Theo's, I mean, Dr. Hornby's, schedule. You might want to check with Dean Miller's office. It's right down the hall to the left."

"Thank you, Mrs. O'Leary. I'll do that. Have a pleasant day." Smith exited the library and as he did, Mrs. O'Leary quietly followed his movement, noticing that he did not turn left, but right, as he left the library.

She returned to the table Smith had been using and picked up the reference volume lying there. "Why would he be researching *Respiratory Ailments in Senior Citizens*?"

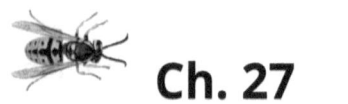 

Ch. 27

Bubba Delvaney had no idea where he was. He knew that it was pitch black, that there was an overwhelmingly putrid smell all around him, and that he felt imprisoned in a spirit of abandonment.

If he was in the hospital, there was no evidence that anyone was coming to his aid. No one.

"Where the hell is everybody? Why isn't anyone taking care of me? And why's it so damned hot in here? Am I having a nightmare?"

Ch. 28

Philip Barton was an adjunct faculty member at FBC. As a graduate student himself, Philip was teaching a couple of science courses for the college. His nickname was "Bugs," for his specialization was entomology, the study of insects.

Bugs was really into insects. "They're a primary food source," he said to his students. "And not just to birds and other animals! Humans are learning that high levels of protein are readily available if one only takes advantage of crickets and locusts!"

His students let out a collective "Ewwww!" "Why would anyone want to eat insects?", asked one student in his Elementary Science class.

"Well," Instructor Barton replied, "there is already cricket flour or cricket powder which is made up of whole dried crickets.The result is a whole protein food. It's sometimes used as a protein powder in smoothies or to make protein bars. It can also be substituted for 25% of the flour in any recipe. And, just so you know, a company called 'Brooklyn Bugs' sells a one pound canister of roasted crickets."

"That's disgusting!", said another student in the back of the classroom.

"I appreciate your perspective, class, but roasted crickets are high in iron and calcium, low in fat, and contain all nine essential amino acids."

"But don't they taste funny?", asked a coed in the front row.

"Granted, they are a bit crunchy. In terms of flavors, one may purchase chocolate coffee crickets, sour cream and onion crickets, honey mustard crickets, curry grasshoppers, and even apple pie or pumpkin spice seasoned roasted crickets. But once you get over the idea of eating insects, it can be quite, shall we say, illuminating."

"What's 'illuminating' about eating a bunch of bugs?", queried another student.

"May I remind you, Class, that John the Baptist consumed locusts and wild honey as he prepared the way for the Lord?"

"I hate to ask this, Sir, but what other insects are, well, consumable?" The disgust on the student's face was shared by most around him.

Instructor Barton replied, "Believe it or not, there are culinary grade manchurian scorpions, also called edible armor tailed scorpions, that some say taste like shrimp."

"But aren't scorpions venomous?", asked the same student.

"Manchurian Scorpions are venomous when they are alive but soon after they die, the poison goes inert and can no longer harm you. A lot of people even eat them whole, stinger and all. Although, most like to remove the stinger before they eat them."

"You asked what other insects are edible, I believe. Black ants, something called 'pizza super worms,' even ant larvae is consumable (and is a regular menu item in Mexico). There are nearly 2,000 insects that are in diets from people around the world."

Barton continued. "When you think about it, there are trillions of crickets that exist at any one time on our planet. And when it comes to ants, there are twenty quadrillion ants worldwide, or 2.5 million for every living human."

The students' shock seemed to be diminishing, as the bell rang for the end of class. "Just so you know, Students, I have some shortbread cookies here on my desk made out of 50% crickets. Please help yourself. Now, let's go to lunch!"

A few students grabbed a cookie or two, but most seemed pleased that the class was over.

As Barton entered FBC's cafeteria, he couldn't help notice that some students were looking at him kind of funny. "Well, I guess that goes with my being nicknamed 'Bugs'," he said to himself.

"Mr. Barton?", asked Dr. Hornby.

"Yes, Professor Hornby! Good to see you."

"And it's great to see you as well. So thankful that you're willing to cover the required science courses for us."

"It's my privilege, Sir."

"Philip, may I call you 'Philip'?", asked Dr. Hornby.

"Of course, Sir!"

"And you may call me 'Theo.' Mind if I join you for lunch?"

"Not at all, Dr. Hornby, I mean, 'Theo.' I was pretty much resigned to eating alone today."

"Why is that?", Hornby asked.

"Well, I gave a bit of a lecture this morning on consumable insects."

"Really? That's fascinating. But I do have one question for you."

"Fire away, Professor."

"Philip, this may sound really strange, but my question is: Can a wasp be weaponized?"

Ch. 29

"You know, standing in the way of God's dispenser of judgment is quite dangerous," John Smith said to himself. "I'm not at all pleased with this Hornby character. I just might have to step up my meeting him."

Smith gathered his backpack and drove over to the campus of FBC. He entered the administration building, passing by the library on his way to the faculty offices. He happened to see Mrs. O'Leary at her desk, talking with one of the student workers. He did not notice that she caught a glimpse of him as he went down the hall.

"Dr. Hornby?" Smith said after he had knocked on Hornby's office door.

"Yes? May I help you?" Hornby looked up at the large man.

"As a matter of fact, I believe you can. Might I have a few minutes of your time?"

"Of course." Hornby stuck out his hand to shake Smith's and said, "My name is Theophilus Hornby, but my friends call me 'Theo.' Who do I have the privilege of meeting?"

As Smith entered Hornby's office, he said, "My name is John Smith and your librarian, Mrs. O'Leary, suggested I drop by to see you."

"Okay. Nice to meet you. May I call you 'John'?"

"Absolutely. I've got a few questions about the degree program here at FBC. I'm considering sponsoring my nephew's first year and I've heard that FBC is a terrific school."

"Well, we certainly hope so. May I offer you what I offer any student who visits me? An RC cola and a Moonpie?"

"That would be terrific, Theo. Reminds me of my childhood."

Smith noticed that there was a cup of tea sitting on a small tray in front of Hornby's desk. As Hornby turned around to fetch the RC cola from his small dorm fridge, Smith quickly dropped a small tablet into Hornby's tea.

After Smith had asked all of his questions about a Freshman year at FBC, he said, "Theo, you've been a tremendous help. Thank you for taking the time to talk with me." Smith shook Hornby's hand, Hornby couldn't help but notice that his own hand was engulfed by Smith's large one.

As Smith walked down the hall, Hornby wondered out loud to himself, "Why didn't that Smith fellow simply go to the administration office with his questions?" Oh, well, he thought. I hope I was some help to him.

Ch. 30

"I have GOT to figure out where I am!", Bubba Delvaney screamed. "I can almost feel the darkness. My brain is exploding with a sense of abandonment. I am completely alone. No one is attending to me or my injuries. The pain throughout my body is excruciating! If I didn't know better, I'd conclude that I must be . . . . can it be? . . . I must be IN HELL?!"

"But hell is a myth! Maybe the hospital gave me drugs that are making me hallucinate. There can't be a real hell. There just can't be!"

Ch. 31

As John Smith left FBC's campus, he had mixed emotions. "I really didn't want to do in that nice old professor," he said to himself. "But he was getting in the way of my work. My divinely-appointed work. And I just can't let that happen!"

Checking out of his hotel, Smith said to himself, "I can't wait for my next assignment! It's so good doing the Lord's work!"

Ch. 32

I'm not taking 'no' for an answer, Mrs. O'Leary thought to herself, as she grabbed a small Tupperware container of her shortbread cookies and a pint of her homemade apple cider. She resolutely headed toward Dr. Hornby's office, preparing her short speech about their "relationship."

"I know he's as lonely as I am," she said under her breath. "And if I wait till he comes around, I'll turn eighty and still be alone!"

As she passed Dean Miller's office, she noticed him opening the door. "Mrs. O'Leary?"

"Yes, Dean Miller?"

"I wonder if you might have a minute or two to talk about the library's budget? I'm trying to put the finishing touches on the administrative forecast for this next school year. It'll take just a couple of minutes?"

Mrs. O'Leary had a strange premonition and decided to act on it.

"Dean Miller, I'm so sorry, but I was just on my way to see Dr. Hornby. Might we have our conversation later on this afternoon? I should be free after lunch."

"Yes, of course," Miller responded. Miller could see the container of cookies and the jar of what appeared to be apple cider in Mrs. O'Leary's hands. Miller was not naive about Mrs. O'Leary's affection for Hornby, and so he let her go.

When she arrived at Hornby's office, she could see that he was sprawled out on the floor, his pointer finger still in his tea cup. "Someone call 911!",

Mrs. O'Leary screamed down the hall. "He's not breathing!"

Ch. 33

Six people were gathered around Hornby's prone body. These included Mrs. O'Leary, Dean Miller, Officer Bondo in a wheelchair, Michael Delganey, and a respiratory therapist. An ER doctor was also on the scene.

As Hornby woke up, the ER doctor told him he was in Bethesda Hospital and had to have his stomach pumped.

"What happened?", Hornby asked the doctor,

"Well, as best as we can determine, you were given a drug that stopped your breathing." He looked at his chart. "Oh, yes. It was benizodine aplacoment, a drug used to induce a coma in a critically-injured patient, but given in very small doses. You ingested three times the amount prescribed."

The ER doctor continued, "If it weren't for Mrs. O'Leary here, you would not have survived!"

"Mrs. O'Leary?", Hornby tried to sit up.

Mrs. O'Leary stepped up to Hornby's bed and put her hand on his shoulder. "Yes, Theo. I found you lying on your office floor, not breathing."

"What did you do?", Hornby asked.

There was a definite blush on her face as she said, "Well, Theo, I had to administer mouth-to-mouth to get your breathing going again!" Those present in the room seemed to notice a slight smile as she reported what she did.

"Let's let Dr. Hornby rest, everyone," the ER doctor said. "You all can come back in a couple of hours to visit with him." Hornby's student Michael looked at him with deep affection, so thankful that he was going to be okay.

Several hours later a crew of four came into Hornby's room. Dean Miller said, "I'm so glad you're alive, Theo! What a terrible scare! However, I did notice a rather large man hustling down the faculty hall this morning."

"That man was in my library doing research earlier today, " said Mrs. O'Leary. "I think he said his name was John Smith. He was looking at a reference book on respiratory ailments of senior citizens!"

Officer Bondo wheeled himself into Hornby's room. "Hello, Theo. Remember me?"

"Of course. Of course. Officer Bondo, thank you for coming to see me."

"Please call me 'Alex.' The room I am in is just down the hall. I heard the commotion as they brought you into the ER and then into this suite. I just had to check up on you!"

"Thank you, Alex. Just so you know, your information about Bubba's being afraid of only one thing really helped me in my little investigation."

"How so, Dr. Hornby?" Both Bondo and Michael were eager to hear Hornby's response.

"Well, nobody in their right mind just drives off a cliff. So I concluded some other person must have been involved in Delvaney's death. The information that you got from the Delvaney family that Bubba was afraid of only one thing and that one thing being wasps got me to thinking! I was able to consult with our adjunct faculty member Mr. Barton, otherwise known as 'Bugs.'"

Dean Miller, Mrs. O'Leary and Michael all laughed.

"Barton knows his insects. And I asked him if a wasp could be weaponized. He did a bit of study and learned that a wasp could be put to sleep but would later wake up when exposed to fresh air."

"So," Bondo said, "how did that information help you, Dr. Hornby, I mean, Theo?"

"I believe that someone put a sleeping wasp in Bubba Delvaney's Lexus and when it woke up, it caused him to drive off a cliff in terror."

"Wow!" Officer Bondo said. "But how does this John Smith fit in?"

"I think he may well have been behind all this. Afterall, he did try to poison me. And he could have messed with your brakes as well, Alex!"

Michael looked relieved that the mystery surrounding his uncle's death was solved, although the murderer was no where to be found. An APB was put out to find John Smith, but he had vanished.

 **Ch. 34**

"Man! That got to be a lot more complicated than I had anticipated!", John Smith said to himself as he checked out of his hotel. "I guess doing the Lord's work can bring its own set of challenges!" He smiled as he left the hotel . . . eagerly anticipating his next "assignment."

Ch. 35

"Say, Theo?", Mrs. O'Leary asked, shortly after the others had left Hornby's room.

"Yes, Mrs. O'Leary. I mean 'Scarlett'?"

"The doctor says you'll be good to go home tomorrow. How's about my bringing over some of that homemade apple cider and a few shortbread cookies to celebrate your survival?"

"That's very nice of you, Scarlett, but . . ."

"Theo, I don't want to say you owe me, but we are more overdue than a stack of musty old theological tomes."